Little pronghorn stops and listens.

What does she hear?

Tweet!
Tweet!

Bison calf
has a little
friend.

Prairie dog pups eat their lunch.

This fuzzy crane chick looks for insects to eat.

Little foal
snuggles
close to
Mama.

Fox kit
explores
outside
his den.

Bunny twitches her nose.

What does she smell?

Skunk kit plays in the pink flowers.

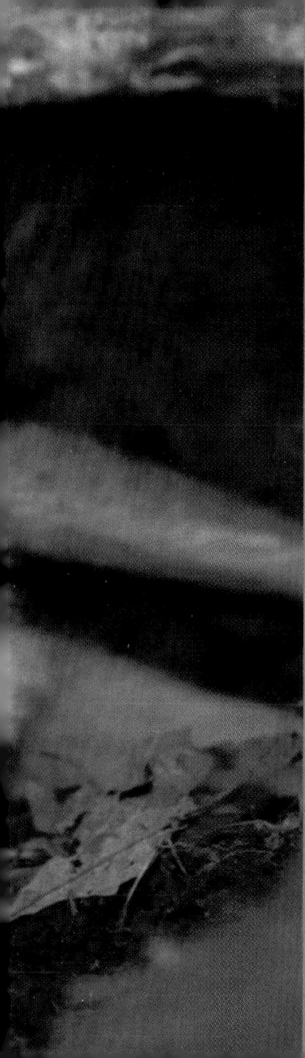

A sleepy coyote pup naps with his mama.

Featuring 10 Prairie Animals!

Woodchuck
Pronghorn
Bison
Prairie dog
Crane

Wild horse
Fox
Rabbit
Skunk
Coyote

Photography © 2003: Lisa and Mike Husar/Team Husar: woodchuck, bison, sandhill crane, red fox, striped skunk, coyote; Michael H. Francis: pronghorn, wild horse; Paul and Joyce Berquist: black-tailed prairie dog; Image Select International: cottontail rabbit.

Designed by Brad Springer

Written and edited by
Kristen McCurry and Aimee Jackson

NORTHWORD
Books for Young Readers
www.tnkidsbooks.com

NorthWord
11571 K-Tel Drive
Minnetonka, MN 55343
1-888-255-9989

Library of Congress Catalog Card Number: 2002043143

Printed in Johor Bahru
Malaysia, May 2016

ISBN 978-1-55971-873-8

UPC 0 52944 15436 3

U.S.A. $6.95
Canada $7.95

ISBN 978-1-55971-873-8
50695
9 781559 718738